The Pierced Rose: Poetry and Short Stories

Holly Hamilton

Ukiyoto Publishing

All global publishing rights are held by

Ukiyoto Publishing

Published in 2022

Content Copyright © Holly Hamilton

ISBN 9789360163853

All rights reserved.
No part of this publication may be reproduced, transmitted, or stored in a retrieval system, in any form by any means, electronic, mechanical, photocopying, recording or otherwise, without the prior permission of the publisher.

The moral rights of the author have been asserted.

This is a work of fiction. Names, characters, businesses, places, events, locales, and incidents are either the products of the author's imagination or used in a fictitious manner. Any resemblance to actual persons, living or dead, or actual events is purely coincidental.

This book is sold subject to the condition that it shall not by way of trade or otherwise, be lent, resold, hired out or otherwise circulated, without the publisher's prior consent, in any form of binding or cover other than that in which it is published.

www.ukiyoto.com

Dedication

This poetry and short story collection are written for the people of Ukraine. May you find peace in a time of war.

To my friend, Darla, without your encouragement, this collection would never have been put together. Thank you, my friend.

CONTENTS

Grandma's Funeral Poem	1
Goodbye Baby Nephew	3
Dolphin's at Play	5
April Showers	6
Covid Mom	7
Memories	9
The Elderberry Witches	11
Forever, Love	14
The Last Salem Witch	24
The Things I Miss	30
Armageddon	32
The World of the End	34
Ukraine, Ukraine	36
For Grandpa	37
About the Author	*38*

Grandma's Funeral Poem

When a petal falls from the rose,
The beauty of color still brightly shows,

The world will hold her memory,
I will think of her in reverie,

As a child, she loved me well,
Her voice was the softest bell,

She loved it when I played her notes,
She loved the poems that I wrote,

When I was a kid we went to Chicago town,
We went to the museums up and down,

When I was sick, she took me in,
She made me smile, made me grin,

She liked to play dress-up with me,
And decorated me with her jewelry,

She lived beside Twaney Lake,
She loved to cook, loved to bake,

As I grew up, I got married,
I had my own children that she carried,

She loved my son and his curls,
She loved my precious baby girl,

She got to know them a little bit,
That is something I will never forget,

She loved people and loved to give,
She taught us all how to live,

Goodbye my grandma, we will miss you,
Thank you for all that you do,

I feel your smile shining from above,
We remember your gift of love,

When a petal falls from a rose,
The beauty of color still brightly shows…

Goodbye Baby Nephew

Heaven received an angel today,
The light of God's grace will forever stay,

I never got to meet your face,
But I know you are experiencing the beauty of grace,

I never got to kiss your head,
I prayed for your life beside my bed,

I never got to see your eyes,
But I think of you in heavenly skies,

I never got to hold your hand,
But somehow, I will love you forever my friend,

I never got to touch your nose,
But I will remember your beauty as a rose,

I never got to hear you laugh,
Or see pictures of your first bath,

I never got to touch your feet,
But I know they were gentle, strong and sweet,

I never got to give you a hug,
As gentle as a ladybug,

I never got to hear your voice,
It would have been the softest noise,

I never got to tell you,
How much I love you,

I will love you forever as your aunt,
To me you were perfect and innocent,

So, fly away beautiful butterfly,
Up towards the heavens, up towards the sky,

Be a gentle angel shining on me,
And know you are cherished by your family...

Dolphin's at Play

I've got to spend this time with you,
Enjoying the world and ocean view,

I've had this time to know you more,
More than I ever did before,

I've slept by the ocean in a tent,
That was time well spent,

I've seen whales splash and play,
In the beautiful Kukio Bay,

I've seen hula and tasted poi,
I've explored the island in joy,

My son has become a stronger swimmer,
The ocean floor will always glimmer,

The dancer's made Mia smile,
We've walked mile after mile,

To enjoy a great day,
Of seeing dolphins at play

April Showers

April showers will bring flowers,
Or so they say,
Today, I will see nothing but the rain,
When the rain of this endless storm pours all over me,
the cold of each drop will somehow set me free,
April showers bring us flowers,
As the house arrest carries on,
Dear April showers I'm at my end, I'm done...
The summer will be here, or so they say,
The future is not looking bright for the month of May,
I'm tired, I'm burned, I'm lonely, I'm broken,
The silence of my storm is has spoken,
April showers please rain down on the dark,
And give us hope, light, a renewing fresh start,
April showers bring us flowers, or so they say,
I'm done with keeping my beloved friends away,
I'm tired, I've tried, I've cried, and cannot carry on...
This house arrest is getting too long,
Wear a mask, and stay six feet away-
April showers will bring flowers, or so they say.....

Covid Mom

In Covid I am all alone,
So I turn to my phone,
I turn to my phone and see,
Everyone's depressed like me,

I can't run and I can't hide,
So I'll make it to other side,
The other side where I can be,
Connected and a little more me,

The other side is where we want to go,
This pandemic has made us slow,
I miss a world with no masks,
Miss my errands and my tasks,

Miss my kids going to school,
Sick of all these health code rules,
Sick of missing all my friends,
Wondering when we will be together again.

In Covid we are not alone,
We are all done with being at home,
Time to get on with our lives,
I want to thrive not just survive...

I'm saying this to help me cope today,
It's a way to help me pray,
For now I will help my kids,
It's the only way I know how to live,

In Covid we aren't our real selves,
Trapped in the dream of someone else,
It's time to wake up my friends,
And never let this happen again...

Memories

COVID 19 you took our plans away
You made us sit down and pray,

Our lives were rushed before the great pause,
We made long schedules, just because...

But now we are stuck... Stuck inside,
Stuck inside with human pride,

This is a chance to start anew,
To give focus, on what is true,

We have families, kids, and schools,
Who need us to follow these hard rules,

But it's hard to know what's right,
When worry takes our joy away at night,

In the morning, I hope we pray,
For our health, day by day,

We stay at home, and we get bored,
When we should cast our worries toward the Lord,

I hope my kids will remember this time,
As a moment when their childhood could shine,

I've had fun learning about them all over again,
This moment will not last, it will one day end,

And when it is all over, said, and done,
I want to remember the laughter, the fun,

I want to remember the sunshine,
Because it will stand the tests of time,

Oh virus, you took our busy away,
So we could rest, enjoy, and play

The fear is real, but so is the love,
And that is a gift from God above

The Elderberry Witches

It was Halloween night 1854. It was the last night I was alive. The last night my breath was ever seen in this world. My parents warned us of the witches that lived nearby. They were the sort of witches that existed in fairy tales.

The Witches of Elderberry. They were the ones who kidnapped children, tortured turtles, and stole faces. And that is what happened to my brother Mark and me. My name is Elizabeth Wilson. I died at the young age of twelve. I hadn't even got my period yet.

I followed the black cat down the river. It was a strange cat, with no shadow. That should have been the first clue, that this Halloween was dangerous and creepy. But I am an unobservant girl. The world is cruel to preteens.

Mark was ten at the time. The shadowless cat caught his eye too. He followed behind, as slow as usual. The cat entered a cave. The cave of the Elderberry Witches. There were said to be thirteen witches who lived and worshipped there.

I didn't believe in ghosts or ghouls. Fairy tales were nothing, but hearsay. Or so I thought. The cat turned into a large plump woman. I remember her name vaguely, she called herself Edith Elderberry. She was the head of the Witch Order.

She determined if the blood of a virgin was ripe for the taking. I am sad to say that this particular Halloween, Edith Elderberry announced us to be her chosen sacrifice.

The Elderberry witches gathered around us and bound our hands with rope. I screamed and kicked. Their enchantments took my mind to the stars. I saw heaven and hell. I saw fire and water. Death was near.

The knives of Halloween are sharp. The stone table of Elderberry sacrifice was covered in blood. The ceremony would make them young and beautiful. It would make them live forever. They stole our smiles. Raped our dreams and took our childhood away.

Edith Elderberry held the knife up to my face and began to say words and enchantments that were not from this earth. Fear was ever-present in my eyes, the eyes of a twelve-year-old.

"This virgin is perfect. Prepare her face and bring me the ax."

The Elderberry witches were known for taking heads and placing pumpkins on top of the bodies. Every Halloween we would rise with the moon, to warn the other children to stay away from the Elder Forest...or ye too would suffer the fate of I, Elizabeth Wilson, and my brother Mark. Be warned to never come to Elder Forest, Virginia or the Elderberry witches will prepare ye and all virgins in their path for sacrifice.

Forever, Love

It's been twenty-seven days since I graduated from Oakwood University. It's been twenty-six days since I last kissed Justin Wordsworth. Justin is my forever love. We've been engaged for two long years. It's been an impatient journey on my part. And a slow commitment on his.

Kyle Colby, my best friend, introduced me to Justin three years ago during our Sophomore University Honor's Banquet. I sometimes think Kyle regrets Justin and I became a couple in the first place. It's not my fault that Justin's lips taste so good. At the banquet, we kept talking and flirting; two hours after meeting him, we were making out in the back of his pick-up truck. We've been a hot item ever since.

Being in love is a beautiful adventure, full of endless pathways and doors. For me, my life is just about to unfold with my upcoming wedding to Justin Wordsworth. Ah, Justin, the reason all the girls swoon, and all the boys grow envious.

Kyle and Justin were roommates for three years at university. I was always interested in meeting him, but for some reason, Kyle decided to become my bodyguard and kept most of the boys away. I love Kyle for his efforts to protect me, but something in him has been different lately.

"Maddie, do you want to get some coffee?" Kyle asks as he pulls a wallet out of his jeans. He's wearing his usual grey tight hoodie that tightens around his back and arm muscles. I won't pretend I haven't noticed his workout routines. He doesn't have a girlfriend, and he's been motivated to get ripped to attract them. But unfortunately, he's turned them all down to pursue his dream of joining the army.

"Sure, Kyle coffee sounds awesome. But all this wedding planning has me feeling burned out. How come all the other girls don't get burned out from all this ridiculous shopping and planning?"

"I don't know, stop planning and let Jessica take care of it. She's still your maid of honor, right?"

"Yeah, she is. I forgot to ask are you bringing a hot plus one to my wedding. You can bring anyone you want."

Kyle hands the barista a debit card and gives me a large coffee. The contents are so warm. It takes the chill in my body away.

Kyle's hand brushes against mine. I feel a slight redness rise to my cheeks. Kyle doesn't say anything and takes a sip of his coffee.

"Are you bringing a date to my wedding?"

"No. I told you I don't date." His shoe scuffs the floor, and his fist tightens. He used to tell me about his crushes, but our conversations have shifted, and he doesn't talk about his love interests.

"Is there a secret man in your life that you want to bring to the wedding," I ask?

"What are you asking me exactly, Maddie?"

"Kyle, are you bi? It's totally cool with me if you are. You can bring anyone to my wedding."

"No, I don't like men like that. I like women very much. The girl I like is…"

He stops talking, and his face is full of redness. He hasn't spoken to me like this in a long time. I almost forget that it's been three years since Jessica dumped him on our annual hiking trip to the Oakwood Forest.

"So, you do like someone? Who is it? You should ask her out."

"I can't. She's in love with someone else. Can we drop this?"

Our eyes meet, and I catch Kyle staring at my lips when they do. The realization causes butterflies to emerge in my stomach. There's a deep tension between Kyle and me. It's always been there, but for some reason, at this moment, all I can do is stare back at his lips.

Kyle raises his hand like he's going to touch my face. Apart of me wishes he would. The unspoken tension between us has bothered me for years, and that tight, squeezing feeling between my legs when he stares at me won't go away.

I've never been in love with Kyle, at least not consciously. But still, that deep tension between us makes me wonder if there was ever a time, we should have crossed the line. With my upcoming wedding to Justin, I don't have time to dwell on what wasn't. If Kyle wanted me, he would have done something years ago.

My phone beeps as a familiar name pops up on my screen, Justin.

Justin: Maddie, something's come up.

Me: Like what?

The three little dots tell me he is messaging me back. It lasts a lifetime.

Justin: We can't get married. I've decided to be with Jessica.

Me: What are you saying?

The butterflies in my stomach that appeared for Kyle turn into a mob of bats panicking in flight beneath my skin.

Justin sends me a photo of him and Jessica kissing. My best girlfriend has run off with my forever, love. My fiancé has turned my world upside down with a text message.

Kyle keeps talking to me. I'm not sure what he's saying, my head spins. Large tears run down my face, and Kyle catches them with his thumb. The touch of his hand on my face burns into me.

"Did I say something wrong, Maddie? Look, I'm sorry, okay. I can always take Jessica as my plus-one to your wedding."

I shake my head back and forth as Kyle hands me a stack of napkins. He doesn't know I've been dumped. It's not his fault I can't form words. Instead, I hand him my phone and let him read the text messages. His baby blue eyes scan the text message quickly as his jaw clenches.

"Want me to kick his ass? I'm going to kill him. Nobody cheats on you, not while I'm around. Where is he? I'm going to his house, and I'm going to kill him. No one cheats on the most amazing woman I know."

Listening to Kyle want to defend my honor surprises me. I knew he would always be there for me. We made a promise to each other in the fifth grade that we would always be there for each other no matter what. Kyle meant those words; he's beaten up two abusive boyfriends for me in high school. If Kyle wanted to kill Justin, he probably could do it. The butterflies come back; what is going on? Do I have feelings for Kyle?

"Kyle, it's fine. I probably had this coming anyway. No one wants to be with a girl like me."

"Stop talking about yourself like that. I can't stand it. Of course, someone wants to be with you like that. Justin is too stupid to see how amazing you are."

The tears on my face are for Justin, the cheater. Maybe I'm worthless after all.

"What's wrong with me? Maybe there's something wrong with me. This keeps happening, Kyle. I get into a relationship and build it up in my head, and then...they dump me, cheat on me, or hate me. At this rate, I'm going to die an old cat lady. Can you take me home?"

"There's nothing wrong with you. Would you stop saying that already? All those guys are idiots. They don't see the real you. You're going to find someone else who won't ever want to leave your side. That's the person you will spend the rest of your life with."

Kyle's voice gets higher and louder as a group of our former college peers overhears our conversation.

"Is that the bitch that Justin just dumped? She was such a brat in college." A tall man says as he laughs. Kyle's jaw tightens again, and his fist pounds the table.

"Hey, asshat, I know you weren't talking about Maddie like that."

"Hi, Kyle. We both know I was talking about her like that. Everyone knows she was Justin's little slut. I'm glad Justin moved on and put it all over Instagram. It serves Maddie right for whoring herself with you. Everyone knows you two fuck each other."

"Maddie and I have never...been together. So, you take that back."

"You mean to tell me you and Maddie don't have feelings for each other?" The tall man tilts his sunglasses down and looks Kyle in the eyes. Kyle's whole face turns red, and he doesn't deny or confirm the accusations coming his way.

"That's what I thought. Enjoy your slut." The tall man with the sunglasses turns his back on Kyle, who punches him in the head.

"Don't turn your back on me. No one says shit about Maddie while I'm around. If you ever try to hurt her, I will come and find you...and I will end you. Get out of here, Jason."

Jason's face is covered in blood. Kyle punched him hard enough, and it's clear to everyone that Kyle is stronger than him. Jason and his friends leave the coffee shop. The manager kicks us out as well for creating a scene. Kyle opens the car door for me and then gets in himself.

The car ride is silent. The events of today have my head spinning. I'm heartbroken about Justin. I was never good enough to be a wife. But why do I always have butterflies in the pit of my stomach when Kyle looks at me with his deep baby blues? The very thought of it makes me blush. I quickly look at Kyle from the corner of my eyes, and suddenly it all makes sense. It's been us this whole time.

"Kyle, thanks for defending me back there. You really didn't have to do that."

"Yes, I did. Justin hurt you, and no one ever calls my Maddie a slut."

My heart skips a beat; Kyle has so quickly called me his. Have I been blind to what's been in front of me this whole time? Kyle slams the breaks as a deer jumps in front of his car. He hit the brake so hard that I grabbed his hand somewhere in the process. I've never held Kyle's hand before. It's softer than I imagined it to be. Kyle doesn't move; he's shaken up from the deer.

"Are you okay?" Kyle asks as he looks at my lips again. The trees around the car create a cathedral of green around us. The wind blows through the open windows, and our car still isn't moving. Kyle's thumb brushes against each one of my fingers. This is new territory for both of us. Kyle pulls his hand away as we both look down at our hands. He keeps his eyes on the road.

"I'm okay. The deer just startled me, that's all." I keep looking at Kyle's hand. This urge to touch it again burns in my mind. My skin longs for our fingers to intertwine. I take the first step and let my hand find his again. Kyle's eyes are surprised, but then his eyebrows relax in approval. He brushes his thumb against all my fingers again. My heart throbs in my chest.

"Maddie, I'm really sorry about what happened with Justin today. You didn't deserve that," Kyle says as he lets go of my hand and parks the car.

Kyle gets out of the car and walks toward his favorite spot, the bench out on the dock. He lives at his parents' house on a little lake. He walks to the bench, and I follow behind. We sit together on the bench and listen to the sounds of water birds and bullfrogs. The sunset is nearing, and it's hard to believe I am not getting married anymore. I've gone from crying to feeling nothing but a dark hollow emptiness.

"Do you really think there is someone out there for me? Or maybe all the good guys are taken, and I am doomed to fall in love with the weirdos."

"Of course, there is someone out there for you." Kyle blushes again. He's been blushing all day, and the thought of it makes my heart jump in my chest again.

"Who? Who in their wildest dreams would want to be with me? There's obviously something wrong with me. I'm defective."

"You aren't defective, Maddie. And I know someone who thinks the world of you." Kyle looks down at his feet and turns his eyes away from me.

This is the moment I've been wondering about our whole lives—the truth about where we stand as friends.

"Who?"

"Umm...well. I do. I... what I mean to say is I think you're amazing."

Kyle puts his hand on my face, and it catches me off guard. For a girl who's just been dumped, I don't feel abandoned. Instead, my best friend has crossed a line today, one that I've always wanted him to cross. An invisible line we have both longed to explore.

"What are you saying?" I ask as my hand finds his. I lean into him and listen to his heart pound.

"I'm saying I'm in love with you, Maddie. I know my timing is off. I should have told you ages ago. But you were so happy with Justin. I couldn't say anything. I was going to be the weird single guy. But I had to let you know just once."

I have nothing to say; there are no words for what I'm feeling right now. So instead of talking, I grab his face and pull Kyle in for our first kiss. His lips are soft and are as familiar as I imagined them to be. The squeezing sensation between my legs grows stronger, and it's hard to hold it all back. This whole time it's been Kyle, and no matter where life takes us, I know I've found my forever love.

The End.

The Last Salem Witch

Dead girls were hanging in large plastic bags from the ceiling the night Vivian Wallace decided to get out her great-great grandmother's ouija board. That was thirteen days ago. It's been thirteen days since Halloween night. On that very evening, I saw the Last Salem Witch appear from the ouija board. She warned us of the terrible curse of the Salem Witch Trials. But like an old wives tale, my thirteen friends and I didn't believe her.

As the sole survivor of such a horrific scene, let me take you back to the very night when all hell broke loose. For if I don't, there is no doubt in my mind that Sarah Good's un-dead resurrected baby, Elisa Good, will haunt me in my dreams forever, and I can't have that on my conscience.

Thirteen nights ago...

It was Halloween night, and nothing could be more boring than pretending ghosts exist. Vivian Wallace bragged at school today that she can channel spirits and ghosts. There's no way in hell that she can convince me otherwise. I've seen enough cheesy movies to know better.

"Emily, get down here. Your friends are here to pick you up for the Halloween party."

Nothing is exciting about Halloween. Even though I'm from Salem, home of the infamous Salem Witch trials, nothing could interest me less than Halloween night. Witches are about as real as the ones from that *Hocus Pocus* movie who sing about putting a spell on you.

As always, I dress in my witch's costume and hat. Vivian has the loudest Halloween parties on record. The cops were called two years ago because her older brother's band played too loudly.

This year, however, is a smaller party. It will be just us girls, and by us, I mean my cheerleading squad. There are fourteen of us, and Vivian told us she has a little game to play when we arrive.

I head out the door and see my friends in their witch costumes. Their costumes are black, purples, and teals. Aren't we a little old to be playing Halloween night?

Vivian greets us at the door as we arrive. A different handshake and smile for each one of her guests.

"Greetings, ladies, tonight I have a little surprise for you all. Before you ask what the game is, gather in my bedroom. It's all set up."

We tiptoe up the stairs, and the steps crack and snap beneath our socks. Our belongings are piled up by the door. Little did we know that going into Vivian's room was the last place any of us belonged tonight of all hallowed nights.

"What is that thing," Janice asks?

"That is why you are all here. This is my maternal great-great-grandmother, Hannah Good's, ouija board."

The ouija board is covered in dust, and the lettering is faded. The letters are red and rustic in color. I blow the dust off and get a little in Janice's eyes.

"Who shall we summon tonight," Vivian asks?

"Your great-great-grandmother, of course," Janice squeaks with excitement.

Janice places her hands on the planchette, and the indicator starts to have a mind of its own.

"Ask who's there," I say, convinced it's a hoax.

"Hello, is anyone there," the indicator moves as Janice asks?

"Y-E-S," Vivian reads the letters that appear on the spirit board.

"Who's there," Ashley asks? All fourteen of us lean in, amazed at the game.

"E-L-I-S-A-G-O-OD. Elisa Good. Oh, that's my great-great grandmother's mother."

"A-S-K-M-E-W-H-A-T-I-A-M. Ask me what I am? Okay, what are you," Vivian asks?

"T-H-E-L-A-S-T-S-A-L-E-M-W-I-T-C-H. The last Salem witch," I say, as my heart pounds in my ears.

Then a tremendous foggy smoke appears over the board, and the planchette breaks in half. The ghost of Elisa Good creeps out of the board with her eyes and hands rising first from the rustic red letters of the spirit board.

"Hello, girls," the witch says.

Five girls faint. The rest of us freeze, and I single-handedly wave at the spirit within the room.

"Come here and listen to the story of where I come from:

It was 1692 in Salem. My mother was a good woman, or so I am told. The people were preparing for the year, and it was cold and dreary. Then the village had the most unfortunate turn of events. The terrible curse of the Salem witches had come. The doctor made several house calls and did what he could, but it was clear that the twitching young girls were bewitched by a demon or a witch. They twitched and hallucinated and cursed the world with their words. And from those words, accusations appeared. Among the accused was my mother, Sarah Good. My mother, you see, was pregnant with a baby everyone thought to be dead. But here I am proof that they were wrong."

"I've heard the stories; you lie. Sarah Good's baby was dead. It was a stillbirth born in the prison cell," Vivian replies, fixated on the ghost of her dead relatives.

"That's what the villagers thought too. But history has a way of twisting its words, my dear. History forgot about me, Elisa Good. History forgot about Tituba, the slave girl from Barbados as well. You see, she confessed to witchcraft, but the villagers let her go. That was their mistake. For she found me in the corner of that prison cell and raised me as her own. She taught me the ways of the witches. And here I am, ready to rise with the moon in full. But to do that requires a sacrifice."

The ghost witch raised her hands and released her curse on my friends.

"*All of ye, but one has affected me,*
Your bloodline is your undoing as you soon will see,
Thirteen girls must die so that I may live,
It's your bloodlines curse that I will not forgive,
Goodbye wicked bloodlines, take your souls away,
And make me walk upon this earth this Halloween day...."

The house shakes, and the lights flicker. My friends scream, and as they do, their breath is taken from them. The witch snaps her fingers, and the girl's throats are slit. All thirteen of my friends have ancestors that lived during the Salem Witch trials, all but me.

It is my doom to pass this story along year after year until I am dead. For if I don't, she will come to get me instead.

The witch summoned ropes and hung them from the ceiling. My friends dangled from the ceiling in large plastic bags. Now I believe in ghosts, and ghosts believe in me. It's my job to remind people every Halloween. The Last Salem Witch is out for revenge. Revenge on the ancestors that took her mother from her.

The End.

The Things I Miss

I miss the world we had two years ago,
No masks, no rules, we could come, and we could go,
Now, we are scared, and don't know what we need,
Some people's guilt is another man's greed,
We stayed home, and tried to comply,
We did our best, as the world passed us by...

But now the schools have mandates,
That some love and some hate,

It's hard to be a mom in the world of new rules,
You either follow them, or don't know what to do.

I've tried my best to be a good mother,
Teaching my kids to love all others,

But sometimes I wonder if it's enough.
The world they are in now is bumpy and rough...

Kid's emotions are hidden behind masks,
Are their emotional needs able to cope with such a task?

I don't know the answer, I don't know the why?
I don't know how to the love the world when reality makes me cry...

I try to do my best, put my health issues at bay,
My kids are the reason I am still able to play...

I am proud of who they are, and proud of where they'll go,
But that does not mean I do not miss the world from two years ago,

I miss the way the world used to be,

I miss feeling healthy and just being me,

The world has always been blanketed in skin,
But right now, I can't hide the ghost from within,

He makes me sad; he makes me mad,
He makes me long for the life I once had,

I try to hold on to the world beneath my feet,
But most of my days I feel tired, worn, and beat

My kids are my pride, my kids are my joy,
I will love them forever, as my girl and my boy...

We will get through the storms; we will get through the rain...
But it's okay to embrace our pain,

This world needs healing in more ways than one,
Without peace, our ways could be undone,

I miss the world we had two years ago,
But the new normal is all I now know...

Armageddon

When mandates are required,
And not complying gets you fired,

I question what is true and what is real,

When parental rights are threatened,
I question the world of Armageddon,

I question what I know and how I feel,

When my liberties are taken,
Freedom before my eyes is breaking,

I question the leadership that doesn't seem to care...

When children are afraid and no longer know what's kind,
It's time to rethink if they are being left behind,

I question the motives that sensor everyone everywhere,

As Big Brother watches and lives on my tv,
I keep my kids safe and away from this scary reality,

I question the reason children are forgotten,

The days are long, longer than ever before,
I miss the days when the news was easy to ignore,

I question the world that tastes so rotten,

When mandates are required,
And not complying gets you fired...

I question where liberties have gone...

When citizens are ignored, what will happen next?
The future of my country is too hard and too complex,

I question why everything has gone wrong...

The World of the End

My laughter has left me today once again,
It's gone somewhere beyond to the world of the end,

I know not where my happiness lies,
Beyond mountains and caves where the sheep go to cry,

In the land of the sheep, people learn how to dream,
They're fed what they're fed, and they drink by the stream,

I once asked a sheep how to jump and how to play,
He showed me his jumps and cried 'Hip hip hooray.'

The thing about sheep is they follow their friends,
They follow their friends to the world of the end,

So, I asked the sheep if I could come along too,
And he let me follow flock one and flock two,

I followed the sheep, and watched how they grazed,
I tried it myself and learned to behave,

I got used to the ways of the sheep,
I was quiet, polite, and didn't make a peep,

The wolves of the mountains came down from their cave,
To make sure the flock knew how to behave,

The wolves had their claws, and made all of the rules,
They told the sheep how to behave at sheep schools,

The sheep that obeyed, had all their wool sheared,
With promises that the world would 'Get better my dear.'

The sheep that questioned the ways of the pack,
We're viciously silenced, their children attacked,
The pack had their claws, the pack had their teeth,
And with their red eyes, they learned to control the sheep,

The sheep that obeyed kept their friends in line,
Something weird was coming it was a matter of time,

The sheep with their horns learned to fight back,
They made the wolves listen, and startled the pack...

So, if you too have been called a sheep,
There's a place among rams, so get on your feet,

When wolves go after the voices of sheep,
Together we stand, in one mighty heap,

Freedom of sheep is what we all need,
In order to do that, we must give up our greed,

When wolves make sheep fight, we are scattered and small,
But together we stand for justice and all...

Ukraine, Ukraine

Ukraine, Ukraine...

The world will never be the same,

Ukraine, Ukraine....

The world hears your cries of pain,

Ukraine, Ukraine...

War has come like falling rain,

Ukraine, Ukraine...

The world knows you by name,

Ukraine, Ukraine...

When the skies fall in vain,

Ukraine, Ukraine...

I don't know how to explain,

Ukraine, Ukraine...

The world knows this is inhumane,

Ukraine, Ukraine...

The world is listening again and again,

Ukraine, Ukraine...

Hope is all that remains...

For Grandpa

Childhood memories embrace,
is the reason I remember your face,
is the freedom we shared when I was young,
the many lullabies you once sung,
the many trips we once shared,
the many smiles that showed you cared,
Childhood memories embrace,
is the reason I remember your face,
is the way I see God's grace,
as you finished your race,
When I was a child you saw my hand,
as a way to love again,
Looking at me like I am three years old,
I am "five going on six" or so I am told,
Childhood memories embrace,
is how I will treasure your face,
I shall never forget the windy city,
or how many times you called me pretty,
Oh, how you loved the music I would play,
You loved me your grand-daughter day by day,
So, thank you childhood memories embrace,
for allowing my grandfather to fall asleep in grace

About the Author

Holly Hamilton

Holly Hamilton loves writing novels in the Young Adult, Chicklit, and New Adult genres. She currently lives in Michigan with her husband, Matt, and two young children. She enjoys going on hikes, drinking hot chocolate, and going camping in her free time. While growing up, Holly discovered her love of writing at a fine arts camp she attended in Indiana. Holly is also a stay-at-home-mother, former teacher, and current homeschool teacher.

www.ingramcontent.com/pod-product-compliance
Lightning Source LLC
LaVergne TN
LVHW041559070526
838199LV00046B/2045